When Jackie and Hank Met

by CATHY GOLDBERG FISHMAN

illustrated by MARK ELLIOTT

MARSHALL CAVENDISH CHILDREN

With love to my wonderful advisors at Vermont College:
Lisa Jahn-Clough, Laura McGee Kvasnosky, Liza Ketchum, and
especially, Phyllis Root—thank you all for being on my team
—C. G. F.

For William
—M. E.

Text copyright © 2012 by Cathy Goldberg Fishman
Illustrations copyright © 2012 by Mark Elliott

Photo credits:
Photo of Jackie Robinson on page 34: Library of Congress, Prints & Photographs Division, *Look* Magazine Photograph Collection, [reproduction number, LC-L9-54-3566-O, no. 7]. Photograph by Bob Sandberg, 1954.
Photo of Hank Greenberg on page 35: Kidwiler Collection/Diamond Images/Getty Images. Photo taken in 1947.

Every effort has been made to trace the copyright holders of these photos. We apologize for any omission or error in this regard and would be pleased to make the appropriate acknowledgment in any future printing.

Library of Congress Cataloging-in-Publication Data
Fishman, Cathy Goldberg.
When Jackie and Hank met / by Cathy Goldberg Fishman ; illustrated by Mark Elliott.
p. cm.
ISBN 978-0-7614-6140-1 (hardcover) — ISBN 978-0-7614-6141-8 (ebook)
1. Robinson, Jackie, 1919-1972—Juvenile literature. 2. Greenberg, Hank—Juvenile literature. 3. Baseball players—United States—Biography—Juvenile literature. I. Elliott, Mark, 1967– ill. II. Title.
GV865.A1F53 2012
796.357092'2—dc23
[B]
2011016405

The illustrations are rendered in acrylics.
Book design by Anahid Hamparian
Editor: Marilyn Brigham

Printed in Malaysia (T)
First edition
10 9 8 7 6 5 4 3 2 1

Marshall Cavendish
Children

Jack Roosevelt Robinson and Henry Benjamin Greenberg
were born eight years and 1,000 miles apart.

Nobody knew these babies would grow up and play baseball.
Nobody knew Jackie and Hank would meet and become heroes.

Jackie and Hank didn't meet when they were children; their lives were very different.

Jackie's family had lived in the southern part of the United States for a long time. His grandfather had been a slave.

Hank's parents had moved to the United States from Romania, a country in Eastern Europe.

One day, Jackie's father left home to go look for work and did not return. So Jackie's mother took Jackie and his brothers and sister to California. They were the only black family in their Pasadena neighborhood.

Hank and his brothers and sister lived with their parents in a New York City apartment more than 2,000 miles away from Pasadena. Hank's neighborhood was crowded with immigrants from many different countries.

Jackie learned how to play baseball in his sandy Pasadena neighborhood. Hank learned how to play baseball in the streets and parks of New York.

Jackie attended church, and Hank went to synagogue.

Some of Jackie's neighbors threw rocks at him just because he was black.

Some of Hank's neighbors threw rocks at him just because he was Jewish.

All across the country, many hotels and restaurants had signs that said NO BLACKS OR JEWS ALLOWED.

The Declaration of Independence declared that "all men are created equal," but some people ignored that. Jews, blacks, Irish, Native Americans, and many other groups were denied the freedom to join certain clubs or live in certain neighborhoods. Black children attended separate schools from white children.

And blacks and whites couldn't play baseball together; they played in separate leagues.

Jackie knew he could make money by playing ball, but in California, the major sports teams did not hire blacks.

Hank had problems, too. The Detroit Tigers asked him to join the team, but some people didn't want Jews to play.

"Go home! Jews can't play ball," those people would yell when Hank came up to bat.

Jackie and Hank didn't give up. The mean words made Hank mad, but he stayed on the team. Jackie kept looking for a job in sports. He finally became a football player for the Honolulu Bears, a team made up of native Hawaiians, blacks, and whites.

Now Jackie and Hank were about 4,000 miles apart.

Jackie and Hank both played ball until the United States entered World War II and they joined the Army.

But Jackie and Hank did not meet in the Army. The Army sent Jackie to Fort Riley, Kansas, for training. Since he was black, Jackie could not play on the Army baseball team or go to school to become an officer. But he stood up for his rights, along with other black soldiers, and spoke out about the injustices in the Army. Soon, the school admitted Jackie and he became an officer.

Hank had already been trained in the Army, so he was sent to China, more than 6,600 miles away from Fort Riley. He, too, became an officer and worked hard to crush the Nazi government in Germany. The Nazis had declared war on most of Europe as well as the United States and were persecuting and killing many innocent people, including Jews and blacks.

Jackie and Hank were good soldiers, but they did not want to be soldiers forever. After they were discharged, the two men took off their Army uniforms and went back to playing ball. Jackie joined the Kansas City Monarchs, an all-black baseball team that was part of the separate Negro League. Hank became a Detroit Tiger again.

Now Jackie and Hank were closer. They were only 765 miles apart. And both their lives were about to change.

Hank's life changed when the Detroit Tigers traded him to the Pittsburgh Pirates. But one thing remained the same: people still shouted mean words when Hank came up to bat, even though by then there were more Jewish players in the Major Leagues.

Jackie's life changed because many people felt it was wrong for blacks and whites to play in separate sports leagues. One of those people was Branch Rickey, the president of the Brooklyn Dodgers. Branch wanted everyone to play on the same teams. Jackie told him, I can be a Brooklyn Dodger.

Branch knew Jackie was the player he wanted. They both knew that when Jackie Robinson left the Negro League and became the first black player on a Major League team, some players would try to fight Jackie, and some baseball fans would shout hateful words when Jackie came to bat or might even threaten his life. Both men knew this decision would change baseball forever, but they also knew it was the right thing to do.

These changes brought Jackie and Hank much closer. And on a bright spring day in Pittsburgh, Pennsylvania, in 1947, the Brooklyn Dodgers and the Pittsburgh Pirates faced each other at Forbes Field. Jackie and Hank would finally meet.

During the third inning, Hank was guarding the first-base line as Jackie strode up to bat.

Jackie and Hank were only 90 feet apart.

And that's when it happened: Jackie bunted the ball, *kuh-thunk.* He headed for first at full speed. When Hank stretched out to field the ball—*wham!* The two men collided. Now nothing separated Jackie and Hank.

"Fight! Fight! Fight!" people in the crowd yelled.

But Jackie and Hank did not fight. They picked themselves up and kept playing baseball.

"Blacks can't play baseball with whites!" people continued to shout at Jackie throughout the game. "Go home!" they yelled.

Hank remembered similar words being shouted at him.

And the next time Jackie and Hank met at first base, Hank said, "Don't pay any attention to these guys. Stick in there."

Jackie later told a *New York Times* reporter, "Class tells. It sticks out all over Mr. Greenberg."

From that day forward, Jackie and Hank were friends. And even though some people still didn't want Jackie or Hank to play ball, many other people did. Not long after Jackie joined the Brooklyn Dodgers, the Negro League ended, and many great black ballplayers became members of other teams.

Jackie and Hank had proved that baseball was about talent, not about color or religion. During their careers, both Jackie and Hank won Most Valuable Player and many other baseball awards.

After Hank retired, he became a manager for the Cleveland Indians. When his team stayed at a hotel that would not allow blacks, Hank wrote to the hotel owners: *If you want my team to stay with you, you have to take all the players.* Because of that, the hotel allowed everyone to stay.

HANK GREENBERG

JACKIE ROBINSON

When Jackie retired, he became a vice president of a large company, but he continued to work for equal rights. Jackie served on the board of the National Association for the Advancement of Colored People (NAACP) and chaired their Freedom Fund Drive to help raise money for civil rights. On one occasion, an argument broke out in New York City between black business owners and Jewish business owners. Jackie got on the radio and said, "It is wrong for any group to use hatred and prejudice to resolve a dispute."

When Jackie and Hank collided in Forbes Field, many people thought they would fight. Jackie and Hank did fight, but they didn't fight each other. Instead, they fought racism and hatred by treating each other as equals and continuing to speak out against injustice. Jackie Robinson and Hank Greenberg were not only baseball heroes—but heroes for the rights of people everywhere.

FURTHER INFORMATION ABOUT
Jack Roosevelt Robinson
(1919–1972)

Jackie Robinson excelled at sports from a very early age. He was fast and graceful, a natural athlete. He played ball in school and in the afternoons when he got home. All the neighborhood kids wanted him on their team. In high school and junior college, Jackie played baseball, but he also competed in track and field, football, and basketball. At the University of California in Los Angeles, Jackie was the first student to star in all four sports. In 1947 Jackie became a Brooklyn Dodger and the first black Major League baseball player. During his baseball career, Jackie won the very first Rookie of the Year Award and the Most Valuable Player Award. He also led the National League in stolen bases and lifetime batting average, and is a record holder for the most double plays by a second baseman four years in a row. Jackie retired from baseball in 1957. He was inducted into the Baseball Hall of Fame in 1962.

Further Information about
Henry Benjamin Greenberg
(1911–1986)

Hank Greenberg was not a great ballplayer when he was young, but he loved baseball and worked hard. Hank practiced constantly in a nearby park, often not coming home until after nine at night. If he couldn't play ball in the park, he practiced sliding in his backyard. Hank played baseball and basketball in high school. After his high school graduation, he enrolled at New York University and played a little basketball. But Hank continued to play baseball in the park and attracted the attention of a Detroit Tiger scout. Hank's hard work paid off. In 1929 he signed with the Detroit Tigers and became one of the first Jewish baseball players in the United States. Hank was a Tiger from 1930 to 1946 and a Pittsburgh Pirate for the 1947 season. During his baseball career, Hank won the Most Valuable Player Award twice and tied for the most home runs in a season. Hank retired from baseball in 1947. He was inducted into the Baseball Hall of Fame in 1956.

Hank's dates

1911 • Henry Benjamin Greenberg is born on January 1 in New York City.

1917 • Moves close to Crotona Park and learns to play baseball.

1929 • Enrolls at NYU, but soon signs a contract with the Detroit Tigers.

1931 • Plays for the Tigers in the Minor League division.

1933 • Becomes a first baseman for the Major League Tigers.

1935 • Named American League Most Valuable Player as first baseman.

1940 • Named American League Most Valuable Player as left fielder.

1941 • Joins the U.S. Army and serves from May to December.

1942 • Reenlists after Pearl Harbor is bombed, serves as captain, stationed in China and India.

1945 • Discharged from the Army and rejoins the Detroit Tigers.

1947 • Becomes first baseman for the Pittsburgh Pirates.

1947 • COLLIDES WITH JACKIE AT FORBES FIELD ON MAY 17.

1947 • Retires from active baseball.

1948 • Becomes manager for the Cleveland Indians.

1956 • Inducted into the Baseball Hall of Fame.

1983 • Named honorary Captain of the American All Star League.

1986 • Hank dies in Beverly Hills, California, on September 4.

HANK'S WORDS

"I wasn't a natural ballplayer like Babe Ruth or Willie Mays, but if you practice the way I did—all day long, day after day—you're bound to get pretty good."

"Jackie had it tough, tougher than any ballplayer who ever lived. . . . I had feelings for him because they had treated me the same way."

Jackie's dates

1919 • Jack Roosevelt Robinson is born on January 31 near Cairo, Georgia.

1920 • Moves to Pasadena, California, and learns to play baseball.

1939 • Enrolls at UCLA and stars in track, football, basketball, and baseball.

1942 • Joins the U.S. Army and is stationed at Fort Riley, Kansas.

1943 • Becomes a second lieutenant in the U.S. Army.

1944 • Discharged from the Army and contacts the Kansas City Monarchs, a baseball team in the Negro League.

1945 • Joins the Monarchs in March, then signs up with the Brooklyn Dodgers, a Major League team, in October.

1946 • Plays for the Montreal Royals, a Minor League team.

1947 • Plays as second baseman with the Major League Brooklyn Dodgers.

1947 • COLLIDES WITH HANK AT FORBES FIELD ON MAY 17.

1947 • Named National League Rookie of the Year.

1949 • Named American League Most Valuable Player as left fielder.

1956 • Awarded the Springarn Medal from the NAACP for outstanding achievement.

1957 • Retires from baseball and begins working for Chock full o'Nuts as a vice president.

1957 • Becomes chairman of the Freedom Fund Drive for the NAACP.

1962 • Inducted into the Baseball Hall of Fame.

1972 • Jackie dies in Stamford, Connecticut, on October 24.

JACKIE'S WORDS

"A life is not important except in the impact it has on other lives."

"There's not an American in this country free until every one of us is free."

LEARN MORE ABOUT
JACKIE ROBINSON AND HANK GREENBERG

Websites

Find neat baseball facts about Jackie and Hank:

http://www.baseballhalloffame.org

http://www.jackierobinson.com/about

http://www.jewishvirtuallibrary.org/jsource/biography/greenberg.html

Watch Hank Greenberg hit a homerun:

http://www.youtube.com/watch?v=zma3RHvXCB8&list=PLC8F8293CF78
2DDC3&index=16

Hear a song about Hank sung by Groucho Marx and Bing Crosby
(with Hank filling in some lines):

http://tenement-museum.blogspot.com/2011/04/goodbye-mr-ball-goodbye.html

Listen to Jackie Robinson's Hall of Fame speech:

http://baseballhall.org/media/audio/robinson-jackie

Read a poem about Hank Greenberg written by Edgar Guest:

http://www.hankgreenbergfilm.org/about.php

Listen to a song about Jackie Robinson:

http://www.mopupduty.com/mp3/jackie.mp3

Read a poem about Jackie Robinson:

http://www.baseball-almanac.com/poetry/po_jack.shtml

Take a Jackie Robinson quiz:

Go to http://www.quizmoz.com and search for Jackie Robinson

Take a Hank Greenberg quiz:

http://www.amuseum.org/jahf/quizzes/hank_greenberg/index-2.html

Books

Read some books about Jackie:

Burleigh, Robert. *Stealing Home: Jackie Robinson: Against the Odds.* Illus. by
    Mike Wimmer. New York: Simon & Schuster, 2007.

Robinson, Sharon. *Promises to Keep: How Jackie Robinson Changed America.*
    New York: Scholastic Press, 2004.

Read some books about Hank:

Berkow, Ira. *Hank Greenberg: Hall-of-Fame Slugger.* Illus. by Mick Ellison.
    Philadelphia: Jewish Publication Society of America, 2001.

McDonough, Yona Zeldis. *Hammerin' Hank: The Life of Hank Greenberg.* Illus.
    by Malcah Zeldis. New York: Walker, 2006.

Selected Bibliography

Allen, Maury. *Jackie Robinson: A Life Remembered*. New York: Franklin Watts, 1987.

Berkow, Ira. *Hank Greenberg: Hall-of-Fame Slugger*. Illus. by Mick Ellison. Philadelphia: Jewish Publication Society of America, 2001.

Eig, Jonathan. *Opening Day: The Story of Jackie Robinson's First Season*. New York: Simon & Schuster, 2008.

Falkner, David. *Great Time Coming: The Life of Jackie Robinson from Baseball to Birmingham*. New York: Simon & Schuster, 1995.

Greenberg, Hank. *Hank Greenberg: The Story of my Life*. Chicago: Triumph, 1989.

Robinson, Jackie. *I Never Had It Made: Jackie Robinson: An Autobiography*. New York: G. P. Putnam's Sons, 1972.

Robinson, Rachel. *Jackie Robinson: An Intimate Portrait*. New York: Abrams, 1998.

Robinson, Sharon. *Promises to Keep: How Jackie Robinson Changed America*. New York: Scholastic Press, 2004.

Scott, Richard. *Jackie Robinson: Baseball Great*. New York: Chelsea House, 1989.

Tygiel, Jules. Ed. *The Jackie Robinson Reader: Perspectives on an American Hero*. New York: Dutton, 1997.

The Jackie Robinson Story. Dir. William Joseph Heineman. Videocassette. Xenon Home Video, 1950.

The Life and Times of Hank Greenberg. Dir. Aviva Kempner. Videocassette. 20th Century Fox Home Entertainment, 1998.